LET THE WHICH OUT

Short Stories by
Vivien Leanne Saunders

Cover design and Illustrations by Vivien Leanne Saunders
Source images all public domain from www.deviantart.com
Proofed and Edited by Vivien Leanne Saunders, George Glass and Daniel Parry

Vivien Leanne Saunders
Visit my website at **https://sivvusleanne.wixsite.com/authorvls**
Printed by KDP Direct

First Printing: 2019
Amazon

ISBN-9781688423060

For Grandma,
whose Witches outnumbered my Which
and
Lowestoft Library Writers' Group,
who are more appalled by my syntax than my
profanity
Cheers, guys.

Fortune Telling is a cognitive distortion.
After considering different perspectives,
you may find that you no longer believe.
—CBT LOS ANGELES

CONTENTS

INTRODUCTION

Each of my proof readers told me, very politely, that I'd spelled 'witch' wrong. I gave them a perfectly good excuse, but they weren't having it.

"Your reader won't know that! They'll see your book and think that you can't write!"

They may be right (and I'd rather that you think that about the title rather than my stories) but if you've made it this far into *Let the Which Out,* I owe you an explanation.

My grandma had an intimidating collection of fairy tales and nursery rhymes that I loved hearing. I also adored the grown-up, 'proper' words that she used. I would memorise them and then use them at school. A murder of crows, browning the meat, shocking the coffee... you get the idea. So when she told me to 'cut your food and let the witch out', I thought that the proper, scientific, grown-up word for the steam in cut food was... the which (it *had* to have an H in it, because steam is soft and H is a soft letter).

It made perfect sense to me for ten years. When I was in college one of my friends kindly corrected me – after spending a lot of time laughing. My grandma still laughs when I tell her the story. Now you can laugh at me too.

I believe in whiches. I love the idea that one misunderstanding can shape a person's belief – whether it's in a word, in the wisdom of a much-loved grandma, or in their own delusion of infallibility.

The stories I have chosen are all about words and misunderstandings. Some of them are humorous, some are perverse, and all of them shape the lives of my characters. Where possible, my characters have no names. Feel free to call them any word you like – and please, please spell them wrong.

VIV

GREEN

Is the Colour of Happiness

THE AIR TASTES LIKE IRON. The trees are too stubborn to buckle under the sun's glare, but the virgin leaves tremble and tear themselves loose. What sweet freedom! They cannot dance in the still, smothered air. Even the quiet indignity of rotting is denied. They can only lay, supine, as the brutal sunlight beats them into dust.

A woman walks in the garden. She is not barren, nor ripe. She is neither sweet with youth or softened by wisdom. She simply *is* – a creature entirely herself, possessed and possessing her being and matter into a marvel indistinguishable from all the other carrion meat.

But no matter. Move on. She has seen what we cannot: the pool of clear water in the heart of the trite façade. She steps forward, sits on the cusp, trails soft white fingers through the water. She has been deceived. The gleaming, dancing sunlight conceals a mire of shit which coats her hand in an oily film.

The swarm bursts to the surface. They gorge themselves on filth. They will feed the birds at sunset, and perhaps the woman's white cat will stay away for another night. He will not starve without her. However many insects the woman crushes against her skin, he will not come home.

It is irrelevant; she does not defend herself. Inaction grants the parasites a delusion of consent. They embrace her flesh – eager, urgent, piercing the meat and sucking greedily until her downy hair is dewed with blood. Well, it has happened before. The air tastes like iron.

Shall we look away? The sight of blood should not alarm us. We shall not weep. The pain will be gone by morning. We will forget. Everybody knows that.

Besides, once she is under the water it does not matter.

She dislikes the way the surface is violated. The irritation passes. She knows the stillness will return, and be disturbed again, and next time she will not have a role in its ruination. Fewer bubbles will rise, and when it is over the stillness will be replete.

The woman slides her hands down her body just as he had. Her fingers are cold, now – fumbling, rough – digging into folds and dragging at laces with growing sick urgency. Her eyes open. She tries not to cry out. It is impossible. The air is forced from her lungs. She cannot push the pitiless water away. It thrusts her body to the ground. She cannot cry out.

Her nails are bleeding when she finally ruptures the stubborn fabric and plunges her hand beneath. It is late – too late – she had known that the second she cried out. Her tears change nothing. The stones slide back into her pocket and nestle against her thighs. They are still warm from the sunlit path. They are growing colder. They rest.

Watch her: she looks up. There was fear in her eyes, but it is fading. Air and sunlight taunt her, but the water is cool, and sweet, and green. It embraces her, gentling her outsplayed limbs and bulging eyes, insect that she is. Her skin is mottled by the weed-choked light. She adorns the dark bed, lays back, closes her eyes.

There are others there. She had felt them shying from his voice, from the breathless gasp of vows and lies and... and ... and...

Poor things. They have heard it all before.

Now she feels their hands brushing against her feet, her hips, her chest. They were white, too, virginal and scoured before the green made them its own. Bright teeth gleam in the sunlight and smile at her -

- welcome – welcome -

- and do not look away. The lake's children dance gaily through their drifting skirts and the barren hollows of their chests. They cling to their stones, their ropes, as if they had never struggled to free themselves. They have forgotten how to let go.

The woman opens her arms. She embraces her sisters. The world tastes of iron – release – revenge. Her body convulses for a moment. The lake is disturbed.

The empty eyes look away. She has seen something we cannot. An oath. A key. A mouthful of glass.

It is best not to look.

Close your eyes.

DUCK

VIVIEN LEANNE SAUNDERS

DUCK

SOMEONE DECIDED TO REPLACE THE KLAXON WITH MUSIC. I wish I could meet that asshole and shake him by the throat. I used to love music, but now it makes my skin crawl. The sound of blaring horns and ringing bells should warn us, not the sweet harmony of a string quartet. But that's just how it is these days. You wake up, the neighbours are scattered in bloody pieces over your nicely mown lawn, and some motherfucker is playing Mozart on the radio.

It must have been eight generations back when the sirens were loud. Back then, the sound was telling you to run – to dig, to crawl, to do *anything* – to get under cover. People would start screaming and shoving at each other as if the bombs cared who got closest to the shelter before it collapsed. There had to be a clever mind behind that one, as well, weighing up the pros and cons. Will the Loft-wafer do more damage than a pack of rioting cockneys? Some of those women used to carry bricks in their handbags. If that Hipster man had landed in England he would have been bludgeoned to death with a designer leather trim.

We don't riot, now. It's not that we know any better. A couple of centuries isn't enough time to fix a boiler, let alone a species. For a couple of years now we've had a bit of a managerial turnover, but we still go home and kick at the fridge door when the bastard won't shut. You know, the stuff people have always done. And we used to watch telly and listen to music, but we can't do that now, because when the sirens go off we have to –

One time, Sid told me they could catch you out by sniffing at the garlic in your breath. Everyone knew that Sid was full of hot air, but one day he didn't come into work. I heard his nametag was found in a duck pond. Nobody ate Italian for a few weeks. It's just how people are, you know.

I tried telling Ellen that it was risky to sleep alone, but she said she'd heard that one before. The secret to a long life, she said, was to drink cider vinegar and to wear a raincoat in the winter. God help us all, but she could be right. The shiny-robed gaudette is still walking among us. Hell, the static in that woman's hair could probably bring down a jet all by itself and eat a satellite for pudding.

I'm not superstitious. Never have been. I never used to put teeth under my pillow, or mince pies under the tree, even though I knew that my parents would give me a coin or a present in exchange. Nobody knows for sure what will happen if they don't drink pickle juice, but I'm damn sure it has nothing to do with ending up in a pond.

Maybe the solution is to be a duck. They're doing alright. After the first few years I started seeing wild animals again.

They're thriving on all the fresh food out there. It's strange – I always thought they were vegetarians.

My radio has started to crackle. They haven't played music for weeks, now. I climbed up the speaker tower to see if it was broken, but I got shouted down before I reached the top. Sturdy things, those pylons. When I was a kid mum told me not to touch them if I didn't want to get struck by lightning. That's how it was, back then. We were scared of things that didn't move.

I never heard the end of that symphony thing with the oboe farting out the tune. I can't remember if it was good or not, but I'd like to hear the ending. It gives you something to think about, doesn't it? While you're clinging to the table legs and trying not to piss yourself it's good to have a bit of culture. That's what makes you human, sophistication and all that.

If you sing any of the warning music at work you get written up. It's 'disturbing', they say. I remember once they played the Blue Danube Waltz. People were whistling it on the streets, babies were crying... it was chaos. I was the only one who laughed. People don't really smile these days unless they've cracked.

Whatever cider-sparked battery you have turned yourself in to won't matter. You don't look any different to the ones who are caught after you've jumped or swallowed or tied the rope. We all go sooner or later. Ellen is the most flammable person in the world, so I figure she'll drown. I like the thought of jumping, myself. Not in front of something, but off a cliff or a tower. I don't get to see open spaces and that very often. They say it's safer to be locked away.

I guess if you're running off to Dover to pack it in then you wouldn't mind so much, but I'd be begging them for death if I was caught. Not their death: mine. Off the chalk like a pretty bluebird, thank you very much, and you can keep whatever you want to peel off the rocks afterwards. Just drop my name badge into work before you leave, or else I'll be written up again. They didn't believe that I was dead the last time, even after I came into work all covered in blood. They made me pull up my sleeves before they phoned an ambulance. I reckon that demonstrates a 'lack of sensitivity', as they say. I should report them to HR.

I don't need the radio. I can always tell when they're coming. I can feel their eyes inside my skull.

I'm ready.

HUNGER

THOSE WERE THE HUNGRY MONTHS. We remember them, not for the wars that were being fought in distant lands, or the passionate love stories that were droning on in the nearby towns, but for the hunger. There was weariness in the air – the tired cry of a thousand people, so sick of battle and so used to the terror of the battlefield that fear no longer had any meaning. They were dimly aware that they should be afraid, and yet they couldn't spend a scrap of their energy in actually feeling the sharp needles of icy terror.

We could taste it on them, the scent of food where none exists, like the ghost of bread outside a closed bakery. We couldn't fly screaming into the battlefield in our usual way, drinking deeply of the coppery spice of terror. We hungered for the meat of it, and there was none to be found. After a month of futile fighting we retreated to roost for this famine, saving our strength and waiting for the harvest to arrive, as it always does. The place we found was nearly deserted– a small valley in the mountains, too high for mortal feet to climb–

and yet there was a tiny hut there. We thought it was deserted until the woman appeared.

I should explain the taste of fear. Some imagine it to be like mortal taste, but really that is only a word. We can't explain the flavour of it, only the sustenance that it gives. There are stronger fears and weaker fears just as there are stronger ales or more potent tastes, but again there is no comparison. A battle fear will feed us for weeks, a single cry being as filling as a banquet. A child screaming at a nightmare will make us feel full, but it is a paltry dish. And then there are the other fears- delectable and delicate. I suppose you can be a connoisseur of fear just as you can with food, and of course some Harpies are. Although we are built to bathe in the blood of battle, some find more glee in the smaller things. The tremble of fear that you feel when you find out a secret, or the fleeting dart that a you might feel before you surrender your body to your lover- these are delicious indeed. But they are rare, and as difficult to catch as quail. You cannot live off them. You will be hungry. But, for some, the taste is worth the hunger.

The woman in the valley did not feel any fear at all. She fascinated us. She seemed as old as the mountains and as gnarled as the trees. We laughed and mocked her for her age, for her limping walk, for her loneliness. We asked her if she was pretty when she was young, or if she had always looked like a turnip. We offered to scratch out her eyes with our claws so she need not see her decaying body rot around her. The usual things that we say to make people fear us. Hungry as we were, we didn't care that we were on her land, or that such a hermit might be beloved of a god. We wanted to taste sweetness again, and here was this woman.

She laughed at us. It was not bravado, she was genuinely amused. We tried harder. We swooped at her. We cut at her arms and legs, watching the watery blood seep into her ragged clothes. And still she laughed until we stopped, nonplussed. We couldn't kill her- she was of no use to us dead. She went back into the house with the pot of water she'd collected from the brook, and we were left alone with our hunger.

The next time she emerged we tried something new: speaking to her. We asked about her family, her friends. She shrugged and did not reply. We offered to kill her children for her, or to desecrate their remains. She laughed again. We could not scare her. Even when we rocked the beams of her house she did not scream. She already knew her days were numbered.

We decided to leave. There was no point in harrying her any more. We flew to the surrounding villages to drink their small fears, the fear of sparks escaping from the fire into the straw. It kept us alive, away from the madness of hunger that our kind falls prey to. And each day we roosted in the valley, making it our home. Once we'd gotten used to the woman's eerie lack of emotion, we found that she was a good companion. She made up stories, stories of lands far away. She never spoke about her own life, but joked about ours and made up tales of our adventures.

Sometimes she played on an ancient wooden flute. We listened with interest. She wasn't good- her breath whistled at each lungful, let alone when she played, and her fingers creaked with arthritis- but the sound fascinated us. She showed us how blocking the notches in the wood made the sound deeper or higher. She showed us how you can make different sounds by smiling or frowning when you play. All these things might sound simple to humans, but to us it was unheard of.

We stayed with her for a few months. It was a strange, peaceful interlude. In that time, we never tasted so much as a breath of fear from her. In the autumn, we decided it was time to return to the battlegrounds. The mud, you see, makes people fear. They feel trapped; they know that if they are struck down they might die the horrible drowning death rather than the quick battle execution. Like I said, the harvest always arrives. Saliva wet our tongues. We took wing and left.

We spent the first weeks of terror in mindless delight, letting our nature control us and drinking in the delicious food along with their hapless, muddied blood. We shrieked and played and danced in the air, waiting for the next morsel to come our way. We felt as bloated as the scavenger birds that pecked at the bones. Yet the woman's voice whispered to me. Once I had my fill of food I left my flock and flew back to the valley. I have lived for thousands upon thousands of years. To find something new isn't just interesting, it creates an obsession. My hunger for information - to watch the woman and find out what made her like that - was greater for the first time in my life. And so I flew.

I reached the hut at sunset and was hit by a wall of pure terror. It was so thick, so dark - like the burned honey that you find in the heart of the hive. I immediately felt my interest wane– this fear had the woman's fingerprints all over it. I hated her, then. She had deceived me. My claws slid out on instinct. I flew down to the hut, hissing between my clenched teeth, and stared through the window.

The woman looked up from the fireplace, hands over her eyes. "Oh, it's you!" She said, her voice quavering, "I was so scared you were never coming back!"

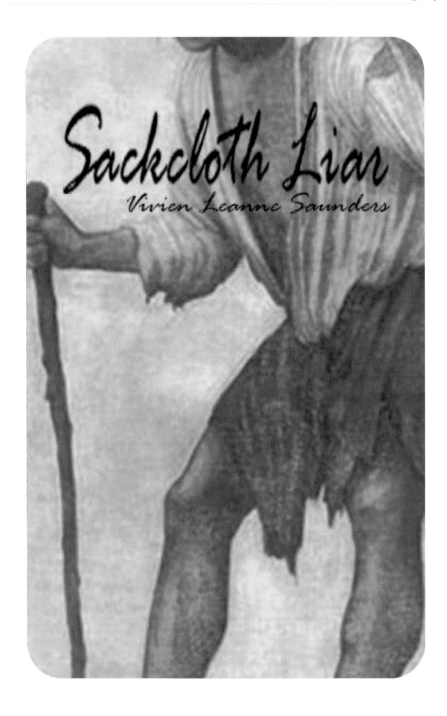

Sackcloth Liar

Vivien Leanne Saunders

THE SACKCLOTH LIAR

THERE WAS ONCE A WOMAN WHO LOVED TO TELL STORIES.

She had six children, and every night she would tell each one a different tale. When they were young the stories were short and simple, but as the children grew they became jealous of one another. They pleaded for more details, and demanded that their story should be the most exciting, longest story of all.

The woman began speaking every night at sunset, and stopped when the sun rose. Her voice grew so weak, and her walk so weary, that all of her neighbours noticed. They decided that she was gentle, biddable and obedient. The woman was too tired to tell them the truth, but every night, bitter about their uncaring ways, she made them into monsters for her children to slay.

One by one, the children grew up and left their home. The woman, now old and haggard from her sleepless years, did not know what to do. Her husband had spent so many years with his fingers in his ears that one day he had decided it was simpler just to go deaf. Her cat mewed and hissed in all the wrong places. She could not reveal her dark, violent imagination to her friends, or they would turn on her.

She cut up her oldest son's bedsheet and wrote his story on it. It was not enough. She could not simply get the words out of her head – she had to get rid of them altogether. So she walked to the coach house and pressed the book into a peddler's hands.

"Take this, and give it away." She begged, "But do not sell it, lest people think they should take it seriously. Stories should be freely given."

The peddler took the book to the next village and gave it to a skivvy in a great house. The servant was so delighted that he pressed a copper coin into the merchant's hand. The peddler, pleased, said, "I walked here. Of course I should be paid!" But the servant was thinking only of the story.

The woman tore up her second child's sheet and handed over his story, "Take this, and give it away. Do not keep it for yourself, for stories should be shared."

But the lazy peddler, content with his copper coin, hid the book away.

The skivvy read the first story to the kitchen maid, who sought out the peddler. "Give me a story of my own, and I shall give you a kiss."

The peddler returned to the old woman, and she gave him the third tale. "Take it, and give it away. Do not trade it, for stories have no substance."

The peddler kissed the kitchen maid, and was so overwhelmed by her beauty that he asked her to marry him.

She said, "You are nothing but a poor peddler! If you prove that you can provide for me, then I shall marry you."

The peddler took the woman's fourth story, and barely heard her warning: "Take it, and do not boast of it, for stories will only ever be made of ink."

Ignoring her, the peddler took the book to a lady-in-waiting and told her that he had written a story so marvellous that it was worth a bag of silver. He showed the money to the maid, and they were married that very day.

Before long, the maid became dissatisfied with her new life. "We sleep in a wagon and eat nothing but sawdust bread! Give me a house, or I shall leave!"

By now, the old woman knew that the peddler was untrustworthy. When he asked her for the fifth story she warned him, "Take this, and do not rely on it! Stories change as quickly as the seasons."

But the man did not listen. He took her story to the prince, who had heard of the peddler's fame. He paid five bags of gold for it, and was so thrilled to meet the merchant that the foolish man puffed up with pride. 'Surely,' he thought, 'I could sell these stories for a *thousand* bags of gold!' So he urged the prince to take him to the king. The prince laughed.

"How can I take you to my father? You're nothing but a peddler! You wear sackcloth and rags!"

The peddler was furious. He took the bags of gold, and the bag of silver, and even the copper coin that the skivvy had given him. He spent every coin on silk and satin, on flashing jewels and gleaming pearls and a pair of gleaming blue boots.

Dressed in his finery, he returned to the old woman and ordered her to give him another story.

"This is my last one," She said, hiding it behind her back, "Do not claim it as your own! Stories can haunt you."

The peddler was so angry that he pushed her away. The old woman hit her head on the mantel and fell down dead. The man buried her in the garden, saying, "I will not need her any more. Her last story will make me rich!" Then he returned to the palace and was admitted into the king's chamber.

By now, the king had read every story his servants had collected. The foolish peddler, in his bloody and muddy silks, opened the sixth story and read it aloud. As he turned the pages he heard for the first time how dark and terrible the woman's stories really were. Trembling, he saw that the king's face was black with disgust.

"You have been spreading filth in my kingdom!" He cried.

"No!" The peddler fell to his knees, "Do not punish me! I did not write it! The old witch in the village sold it to me!"

The king sent his soldiers to the village, but all they found in the old woman's house was a freshly dug grave. They searched the peddler's cart and found the story that he had hidden away. The peddler was dragged out of the palace, marched onto the gallows, and hanged.

Afterwards, the king opened the second, hidden story and began to read. It was just as bad as he had feared. He threw it into the fire with every other book, and watched the first page char:

Once upon a time, there was a woman who loved to tell stories. She had six children...

KUBANDA

UMLILO

VIVIEN LEANNE SAUNDERS

KUBANDA UMLILO

Cold Fire

By the sun who warms us and the river that sweetens the land, raise your hands and we shall name the faces of the stars –

Silalela	*Sifunda*	*Ukithi Siphila*
We listen	*We learn*	*Together we live*

SHE WAS ONE OF THE *IMBONGI*, my family, one who carries their fate in the palms of their hands. She was one of the people of the heavens, under uThixo and above the dust of amaDiozi, who we mourn and fear. She was the daughter of a gracious mother and a father whose ubunto acts were known to the amaZulu, the Nguni and the Swazi. Her eyes were clear and her skin as dark as the shadows of night. She wore brighter beards than the birds, and how she laughed! The girl smiled when she should cry.

All she knew was laughter. *Silalela!*

My sisters, she covered her body, but the men of her village looked away.

"Pah!" They said, "She is impure! Her spirit has no breath. What has she given us but laughter? What will she ever take but joy? Cha!"

Ukithi Siphila!

My brothers, what could she have done to turn their heads? She sang to her idlozi ancestors, but they did not answer. The offerings of salt and smoke made the muthi turn to dust in her mouth. She spat it out and left her prayers unspoken. The spirits would not guide her.

Weep for her! Aya! *Sikhala!*

The wise inyanga heard her cries and pressed his palm to her heart. "It is cold," he said, "You must warm your heart before any man will desire it."

"Yebo!" She cried, "Then that is what I shall do!"

Then, my mothers, she left her home with only a bone knife, amasi curds and the beads around her waist. Her family tore at their robes and screamed. They had only taught her laughter. Now they were afraid.

Sikhala! Silalela!

The girl walked for six days and seven nights until a thorn pierced her toe. She sat upon a flat stone to suck it out. As she closed her teeth around the barb a great cry rang out, and she found that the barb was too strong to be pulled.

"Cha!" She cried, "What am I to do? I cannot walk forwards or back. Must I crawl on my belly?"

So she lay down, and crawled. The snakes streamed out of the stone, but they did not bite her, for her heart was as cold as their own. Her beads broke away from her hips and lay in the dust.

"Yebo, here is an offering!" the snakes cried. They wrapped themselves around the beads until they stuck to their skin and made their scales as bright as bird feathers. So happy were they, that the strongest of them pulled the thorn from the girl's foot.

"Thank you, sister Inyoka." She said, for she knew that snakes did not offer acts of ubunto lightly. Her heart warmed a little in gratitude. The snakes reared back.

"You are not one of us! Go back to your own kind, or we shall bite you with more than thorns!"

Yebo, Sifunda!

The girl was thirsty from her long walk, my friends. She followed her nose to the green amazi Usutu River. As she drank, she heard a great cry. A fish leapt into her hands. It did not fear her, for he thought she was as cool and heartless as water.

"Help me, sister!" it cried, "Cut this thread from my throat!"

The girl drew her bone knife and cut the fishing thread away. Her heart raced and warmed in sympathy, and she held out the blade, "There will be more hunters tomorrow, little brother Inhlanzi. You need this more than I."

The fish took it into his soft mouth and sucked until the carved bone became sharp, jagged teeth. "I should bite you, first!" he shouted, "For you lied about being as cold as my river! You are not one of us! Go back to your own kind, or I shall bite you with more than thirst!"

Hunger forced the girl to stop for a third time. She crouched down and swallowed every drop of amasi that she had carried from her mother's pot. As she finished she heard a great cry, and saw a huge spider scurrying through the dirt.

"Wicked girl!" The spider cried, "You gave your beads to the snakes, and your knife to the fish. Why did you not save a single drop of amasi for your brother Anansi?"

The girl's heart grew hot with anger. "Why should I hurt, and thirst, and starve for those who will just turn and bite me?" and she raised her foot, ready to stamp down the spider if it should bare its teeth. As she did, a high ululation rang out, and a stranger leapt forward to cut the spider in two. He saw the girl's burning eyes and flaming cheeks, and knew that her heart was as strong and fierce as his own.

"I saved you," he said, and he was the first man who did not look away.

What did the girl do then, my brothers? Her body burned like the sun, like fresh coals, like the blood of mountains. My sisters – do you know? Her tongue was wise with the sly words of snakes and spiders. My mothers – do not smile. You already have the answer. Aya, yabo! The girl embraced the man, and together they burst into flames.

Sifunda. The world has burned a thousand times and more since then.

Ukithi Siphila

NO, I...

A THOUGHT AS FLEETING AS A FOOTPRINT
The mark so dead and odd,
Something of man, which no man can claim...
For who can recognise his own tracks?
...and yet it's terrifying; tragic
That the snow should fall so
so slowly the marks disappear.
...something so impersonal, yet unique,
The only trace that this moment passed by,
That yes, for an instant, here was I
A person! Alive, standing in the snow
A moment of life; time irreversibly spent,
Completely forgotten by snow's descent

by divine rite
Vivien Leanne Saunders

BY DIVINE RITE

IT IS EASY TO BE LOVED

It is far easier to be loved by a god. It was almost too easy – as Kernunnos knew all too well. It preyed upon his thoughts as he crept closer to the Beltane fires, and it troubled him.

Many gods stalked the mortal realms on festivals, summoned by the crude rituals of renewal which the mortals scratched out of their ancestors' stories with every poor harvest. How many ignorant girls lay in the dirt, their blood spilled by desperate men whose frenetic rutting hid sordid lust beneath the stink of incense and the tuneless droning of hags? Yet those were the rituals of the seed and the earthen womb. The gods which they summoned were bound to the rites and sacrifices however much they were perverted by the darkest of mortal whims.

Kernunnos remembered the purity that had come before, when the smoke smelled of burned antler velvet and apple blossom. Now his flaring nostrils smelled only flesh, but he was still forced to obey. He balked at their demands. Despite the compulsions which their chanting forced into his heart he fought to turn away from their fires.

At Beltane he prowled the mortal realms with his loins aching, his ears tortured by the thick moans of the women who called his name in their delirium. He saw other gods, his brothers and sisters, creeping into the darkest eyes and sinking into the warmest flesh. It would have been so easy to copy them, to renew the land in a few beastlike thrusts and spill his blessings into some gasping mortal shell, but some part of him detested the idea. His nature was so perfectly poised between human and animal that didactic contest was normal; while the beast in him growled and hungered, the human drew him back, and for many decades the human was allowed to win.

Having rejected lust, his instinct drew him towards the pursuit of other prey. He was a hunter who had learned to respect antler and boar tusks; any prey could turn and attack, and through the centuries the god had gathered wariness about him with every scar. What was this new prey to defend itself with? He watched them as the years drifted past, seeing women whose words were as sharp as talons and men whose adoration stagnated like a seeping wound. Of all he found much to love, but his trysts were over as soon as the snows fell. The mortals hid from the forests, and even the trees forgot them until the spring. Kernunnos left his paramours in the cold and turned his heart to the new year, and before the snows thawed he barely remembered their faces.

He stopped searching after half a century, and slowly returned to the rites which he had so abhorred in the years before. He watched the new generations and his heart turned cold. They all loved him, in their small and selfish ways. If all they demanded of him was an hour of his time, a chance to subjugate themselves under his feral, ruthless body, then so be it. He felt an indifferent pleasure, nothing more, and took the sacrifices of innocence and wantonness with the same blank brutality. For fifty years he only demanded that they did not tell him their names, nor show him their faces. He took their bodies in the roaring firelight with the demanding, silent ruthlessness of the stag.

Kernunnos did love them, for all of their selfish ignorance. They could not conceive of being unloved; they took it for granted, and only resented it when they thought it was gone. In turn, their devotion called him to them. For generations it was enough, and the animal in him was content, and he forgot that he had ever yearned for anything better.

* * *

Hestia was not intended for sacrifice. The god's eye had already fallen upon the other girl they had chosen. He could smell the musk of the leaves in her oily hair and the spices and sex on her skin. She was drunk or drugged, as some of the offerings were – some of the priests disliked risking the most important ritual of the year on some maidenly shyness; some of the women preferred to pass the night in a haze. This girl danced from man to man with the sickening dizziness of one captivated by the senses alone.

Kernunnos felt a heady richness in the cool air, and he drew back into the shadows to watch. Every one of his footfalls was silent, and he did not stir a cobweb from the trees. The girl laughed by the fire, and the goddess in her screamed out her own feral glee. Kernunnos took another pace back into the forest. He had no appetite to feast upon the same altar as his sister tonight. Let her have her lust and her revels; his rites demanded the mortal's bodies, not their sanity. Feeling cold disgust sicken his stomach against the fresh raw meat of his last kill, he was about to turn away when he saw something else.

A girl ran into the firelight. Her face was twisted in anger and her dress was old and patched. Clearly, she had not meant to join in the dancing. It seemed that she could not bear to watch the other woman's ruination. Ignoring the drunken jeers of the other villagers, she dragged the girl away from one of the priests.

There she held her still until the mania eased. As the sacrifice's laughter turned into frightened tears, the goddess streamed out of her like velvet smoke and drifted into the heat of the fire. The patched girl looked puzzled for a moment, and then shook her head. Glaring at the people around her, she helped the other girl up and marched her away from the firelight.

The next year Kernunnos returned to the same village. He had to admit that he was intrigued; the girl had somehow known that the goddess was there. It was rare for a mortal to see so clearly, and yet still follow the primitive customs of her tribe. He found an outcrop of rocks from which he could see the clearing.

He didn't even need to look at the fire. The girl was crouched in his hiding place. She was wearing a finer dress this time, and her golden hair was brushed out and braided with ribbons, but it was obvious that she didn't want to join in the dancing. She was spying on the villagers with a cross expression on her face. The god might have told her not to worry –the goddess was not there, and her choking perfume was half a continent away – but it was not in his nature to make the first sound.

The girl looked around and gasped in shock. Her angry eyes swept up and down, and she pointed scornfully at his head. "What kind of costume is that? This isn't even deer country!"

Kernunnos could not fashion a response. He could have told her that there was a herd of deer less than fifty miles away, but he vaguely remembered that mortals saw that as a large distance. He touched his horns, remembering the crude crowns the mortals sometimes made to wear at the fires, and smiled ruefully, "I've come from a long way away."

"Then keep walking. There's nothing here." Her voice was curt, but polite, "The big fires are in the next town over."

"I know." He smiled when she scoffed and folded her hands. She was acting as if he was bragging. In all honesty he could feel the heat of those fires burning in his heart as strongly as his own aching curiosity. Instead of responding to her mockery, he looked over at the fire where the villagers were starting to dance, "Why aren't you down there?"

She shrugged. "Tomorrow I'll be nursing their sick heads and sore stomachs. It doesn't make me want to join in. I don't think the gods will notice one less dancer."

"You never know who the gods are looking at." He told her, and she smiled at him. It was an odd, bright expression which spilled from her blue eyes like light.

"Well, if they're looking at me then I don't want them to see me drinking myself sick. They must be pretty strange gods if they think that's worth looking at. I wonder why the priests think the gods watch something as messy as that."

The god laughed, and shook his head in some amazement, and when she looked back at the fires he faded into the trees.

As he carried out his duties that night his mind kept bringing him back to those bright eyes, and he missed as many shots as he struck. He thought the memories would fade as he made his way back into the divine realms, but even as he stalked the cool glades of the forests he called home he could not forget her words. Each one lingered, and the snows fell and melted and he still remembered her. How could he? How was her smile more meaningful than any arcane rite? And yet he could not help it. He wished he had said something else, or lingered, or simply stepped a little closer to her.

Do you want her? The sky taunted him. Sometimes it was his own voice. That was bad enough, but when his sister of the wanton arts started calling out to him he had to block his ears and banish her from his lands. She came when beckoned, that siren of the flesh, and as often as he sent her away he called her back with the heat of his dreams or the longing of the long hours. He cursed, shouted, even fought the witch in his anger, but her laughter cut him like a blade.

The next festival never seemed to arrive, but when it did Kernunnos's heart raced so fast that he could barely think. After so many centuries he could not understand this feeling, and he was as angered by it as he was excited. He desperately wanted to forget the girl, but his feet found their way to the clearing and he froze, captivated, at the sight of her.

The goddess had reached her first. Of course she had; she could slip through the realms with the soft ease of sliding between silken sheets. How she must have crept along the girl's body, brushing her skin with soft, delicate promises before kissing her forehead and binding her to her calling. The mark blazed on the girl's head under the crown of leaves and flowers she wore, and the women around her laughed and lead her over a path of willow vines and dock leaves and petals. They took her to the firelight, and she stepped up to a large flat stone as they poured honey and oil over the small, crude statue of their god.

For the first time he could remember, Kernunnos did not know what to do. He could not remember ever wanting a mortal so badly. He saw the silhouette of her body as they drew her shift away and anointed her with blood and honey and made the markings which offered her to the gods. To *him*.

She was beautiful, but that was not all. He wished that it was all, so that he could leap across the clearing and take her right there with the blood of the fresh kill still warm on her skin. He fought the desire, struggled against the beast, and managed to make himself see the things the goddess concealed.

He saw the calluses on the girl's hands and the worried lines between her eyes. He smelled acrid medicines which she had brewed for so long that their stench bled from her skin. Beneath that there was the dull fragrance of death that all mortal creatures carried. He saw the hazy blackness masking her blue eyes, and he forced himself to understand the frightened tremors in her hands and lips.

Detestable mortals! Even the girl that she had rescued was standing nearby, laughing and scattering delicate petals into the stinking mud. The healer was the most precious creature they possessed, and she too was to be spoiled. How could they be so cruel?

It was all for him, this offering. He loathed it as much as he ever had, but he had been summoned here, and so he stepped into the firelight. They took a step back when they saw him, and he let them see him as he truly was. His eyes were burning, obsidian coals, and divinity scoured his face like harsh sand, making it frozen and cruel.

"Leave." He growled, but they were frozen in place. He gathered the girl up in his arms and carried her into the forest. Her heat pressed against his skin and his resolve wavered even then. Setting her down, he glared into her unfocused eyes and had to look away, afraid of what he might do.

"Don't you want her?" The girl's mouth moved, but it was not her voice which spoke but something richer, huskier, the voice of a harlot coaxing a lover into her bed. Kernunnos cursed and shut his eyes. He felt a soft hand creeping up his thigh, the languorous fingers torturing him with their lightest touch, caressing and coaxing.

"No." He croaked, and then he repeated it again with more command and opened his eyes. The girl had not moved; she had passed out. The goddess sat between them. Her full, naked breasts were painted with the same crude markings as the girl's, and she smelled of blood and honey. The goddess had no name, but every name belonged to her once it had been moaned from gasping lips. Tonight was her festival as much as his own, for without her wanton insanity the hope of renewal would soon be smothered in shame. Kernunnos knew her well, but she was too fickle to pay any attention to the gods who thought clearly. Now she pressed closer, and slid her hand between his legs and smiled as she caught his earlobe between her lips.

"You want her." She moaned it into his ear, coaxing him to madness with her hands and her scent and her shallow breathing. He tried to push her away, but his hands sank into nothing but perfumed smoke. She laughed and shook her head, the sprite of desire and restraint split in two. She drank the sacrifices of wild abandon, of sleepless nights in starving passion, and the hunter god finally desired a mortal enough for the goddess to infect him with her madness.

"Let's work together." She murmured, drawing his hand onto the fullness of her breast and parting her lips in a moue of pleasure. "Let me have your lust, dear one, and I will bless this land at your side."

"I don't want you." He told her even as the hunger took him and the beast inside him roared. The goddess laughed, and he turned to her to find that she was gone. His hand was pressed against mortal skin, and the girl was soft and fragile in his arms, and it would have been so easy. He knew now, though, that this was not truly her. The girl he had dreamed about smelled of medicine and had faced him with defiant wit. It was the smoke and the offering that had poured the dizzy liquor of the wanton goddess into her blood.

He snatched his hand away, and it was as if a spell was waiting to be broken. His voice was choked, and it took him a moment to clear it.

"I don't want her." He said it clearly, rejecting this offering to the sky, and felt the curse of the land accepting his refusal. It would be a poor harvest, a bad hunting season and a difficult winter, but he had made his choice. The goddess nipped at him playfully and her scent drifted away; as soon as his heartbeat had slowed she had grown bored and forgotten her desire. Such was her nature.

The mortal girl opened her eyes, but she seemed to think that she was still dreaming. She looked up at his forbidding divine form with no fear. He carried her to the lake and washed the runes from her skin, feeling his ties to her breaking away as each sigil disappeared.

"Why did you do it?" He asked.

"Someone died. They blamed me." Her words were sleepy and simple, as if she thought he must already know the answer and was reminding him. "They said that if I did this they would let me keep my home."

"A few sticks of wood." He snorted, thinking less of her. She shook herself more awake and glared.

"My ma and da built it. I was born there the day my mama died. They have no right to burn it."

Kernunnos made a noncommittal sound and scooped up a handful of the clear lake water. It tasted metallic. The silence did not confuse the girl; with that peculiar insight she had shown before she understood his mood and explained: "They need the farms to do well this year. We're low on grain stores and for two years the harvest has failed. I guess I eat as much bread as anyone else, so maybe I did it for that, as well."

"Learn to hunt." He offered, and was stunned when she laughed. How dare she mock him! Then she turned her face to the moonlight, and he saw that she was simply enjoying her own thoughts.

"I'm a healer, not a hunter. I gather berries but not enough for everyone. Others try but they don't know which ones are poison. Ellen died because she wanted mushrooms, and she thought they were all the same, so she picked the biggest ones because she was hungry." For the first time the girl's detached, sleepy expression faded, and she looked as serious as she had when she pulled the girl from the fire. "She died from ignorance – her own, but also mine for not knowing the antidote – and she died from hunger. If things carry on as they are she won't be the last person to die. It's right to offer myself for a chance at fixing that."

Her pragmatism astounded him. He had refused her offering already, but now he felt slighted – no, offended! – by her callousness. As much as he disliked the ancient ritual, he respected its motives: the pairing of flesh and forest, desire and hunger and the thin light of rebirth flickering amongst the darkest paths of the human imagination. There was a poetry in it which was his law – and whether he admired it or abhorred it, it would always bind him.

But here – this woman – described the ritual like a tradesman selling goods at market. Her goods were sound: she surrendered herself willingly, if not happily, and had followed the ritual to the letter. It was not her fault that he had turned against her. He could not fault her, but he would have rejected her again for her callousness had he known. She believed in her patron god completely. She just did not love him.

"How does... the blessing... how does it work?" She asked him with the first hint of uneasiness in her voice. "I agreed, and they gave me wine and told me that when I woke up it would all be over. I tasted something else in the wine."

The god pointed at the water which had washed all of her markings away. "The river took it."

She blinked and then shrugged, accepting this impossibility as easily as she had told him her story. "Then, I am awake. I'm fair sure whatever is going on, we haven't finished."

He was silent, and the girl's bright stream of words faded away. She looked around and then raised herself out of the water, shrugging off her nakedness with the resigned indifference of a healer. Just as her faith was simply trade, Hestia's body was simply skin.

"This is Whitestone Lake." She spoke slowly. "I know this place. Why are we here?"

"I took you away from those... people." He stopped himself from using a crueller word, but she heard the anger in it and looked puzzled.

"Weren't they just doing what you wanted?"

He laughed at that, and the mortal girl took a step back. Her fear made no sense until the god realised that she did not understand the joke. She had been confident before because she had thought that every moment of her bargain had already been planned. She had known what to expect – but he had broken the rules, and now she had no idea what to do next.

"Have you ever been in love?" He asked her. She shook her head, eyes wide, and the god laughed again. "I envy mortal love. I love easily, and completely, and painfully, and then it fades. I love mortals who die before even a century passes. I forget my lovers who live for years. I love every person that your priests tell me to love, and every year they bring me more of them. They do not feed my heart, but my pride. Would you want that, little mortal?"

She shook her head, but her voice was stubborn. "My name is Hestia."

He bowed his head a little. "Hestia, you did not answer my question."

"Bless the fields and maybe I will." She replied, unfazed by his speech. "People will die if you don't."

He knew that people died anyway – it was only a matter of time – but he suspected that this peculiar creature would scold him for saying such a thing.

"Your offering is not acceptable to me." He said stiffly.

The girl looked down at her naked body, her face set in the same pragmatic scowl that she had worn when she bartered with him. Then she looked up and examined him with the same careful attention. His eyes had followed her own, and by the time she looked back up at him he had to resist the urge to hide his arousal. There was no point trying; they both shrugged off the lie that he had told and smiled ruefully at each other.

"If you don't want me, then at least give me some clothes." She gestured again to her nakedness and laughed brightly at his expression. "You can forget me as soon as you like, but I reckon you'd remember where you lost your best cloak."

"So now you want a blessing and a gift?" He retorted in the same tone. "What's next: a pile of gold?"

"Would you give it to me?"

"Wishes always come in threes. You've only made two."

"But you're not a Djinn." She reminded him, smiling. Accepting the cloak which he handed out to her, she looked as if she was going to continue teasing him, and then her voice grew serious. She didn't sound hurt or offended, but simply confused: "I wish you'd tell me why you don't want me."

"I do want you." He explained bluntly, "But you'd have to want me, too."

"I want you." She said it too quickly and blushed when the god rolled his eyes.

"You want only what I can give to you."

"Oh, and I had a whole drunken evening to get to know you! How far did you expect me to get?" She huffed in exasperation. He smiled thinly.

"The others..."

"The others! What did they do, lie back and open their legs?" She sounded scornful. "Do you want me to desire *that* from you? You'd do just as well finding your precious offerings in a whore house!"

He reddened and struggled for an answer. Finding none, he instead looked up at the sky and saw the first glimmerings of dawn. He had spent the whole night arguing with this wretched mortal, and he hadn't answered a single prayer or blessed a meter of land.

"I have to go." Kernunnos looked into her defiant eyes. They were the brilliant blue of the sky through verdant forest leaves, and he struggled to look away. "I shall return here tomorrow, for my cloak."

She watched him disappear into the trees and her scowl deepened. "Fine! I guess I'll just walk home!"

To her amazement the god laughed, and her eyes were dazzled by a strange glimmer of silver light. She dragged them open expecting to see the rise of the village before her, but she was still beside the lake. Only the odd colours of the dawn light greeted her. She was about to shout something even ruder after the god when she noticed soft fabric under her feet. She looked down and saw the most beautiful kid boots tied to her feet, and soft gloves which fit her hands perfectly. The hunting garb under his cloak was also lined with fur, as warm and as beautiful as that which the lords wore in their mountain keeps.

Hestia smiled, hid the expression from the watching forest, and turned to walk home.

It was a compulsion which drew Kernunnos to Leíthin the next night. Already, the fields were starting to turn: the altitude had coaxed in a bitter wind, and many of the wheat husks had been shocked by the cold. They would rot when they warmed up, and would be useless even as seed for the next year. Kernunnos saw it all with a shade of uneasiness. Now that there was a day's work between himself and the fires he saw his choices for their stubborn pride. He had quarrelled with his sister, nothing more. If he had been negligent it was her fault as much as his own. Not that there was any blame to lay at his feet. If he chose to curse, then it was his divine right. He repeated this to himself as he returned to the side of the mortal, and did not admit that she had captured his mind beyond any petty pride. Naturally, he was only climbing the mountain to retrieve his cloak.

She had washed it, and dried it in air which smelled of lavender, and she held it out to him with a shy smile the moment that he stepped towards the lakeside.

"There." The mortal said, and her smile trembled a little. "You didn't even have to ask for it. If you turn around now and keep walking you could forget me in a few hours, just like you said."

He scratched his chin awkwardly, forgetting to even look at the bundle of cloth. It smelled of her. He would remember her every time lavender bloomed. Kernunnos forgot that he was proud and strong and wronged. He shook his head, watching her shyness as she lowered the bundle, and then he reached forward and kissed her.

She raised her hand to his cheek and her fingers were light against his skin, and the kiss was never anything more than sweet and shy, and as soon as Kernunnos realised what he had done he blushed and pulled away. She kept her hand on his cheek, gentle and soothing, and drew him down to rest her forehead against his own.

"I thought about what you said." She murmured. "Who was the last person to really know who you are?"

He shook his head. Hestia drew back, and her eyes were full of pity, not love. Pity was something else mortals had never felt for him. They were usually too concerned with their own short lives to do much besides envy the immortals. This woman had death following her just a few years away, and yet she looked at him with complete empathy.

That night they walked all the way around the lake, helping each other over the more difficult trails and sharing every thought that came into their heads. Kernunnos did not speak of his duties or the tasks which he was neglecting, and Hestia did not ask. Without the perfumed goddess haunting their every touch they found an easy companionship which demanded nothing from each other. After their kiss Hestia had taken his hand, and it felt simple to walk with their fingers entwined, more like children than adults, more like friends than lovers. They did not try to kiss each other again.

"The festival ends tomorrow." Hestia said when they found themselves back beside the discarded cloak. She picked it up and brushed soft white sand from its folds. For the first time since they had begun their long walk together, she looked at Kernunnos and seemed to remember that he was a god. Her fleeting look of awe turned into a wry laugh as she held out the cloak. "I should have known you would prefer this offering. Do you only accept things that you already own?"

He looked at her narrowly and pushed the bundle away, his words icily formal as if the last hours had never happened. "This offering is not acceptable."

"Acceptable!" She cried, and threw the cloak into the dirt. For the first time, Kernunnos understood that he had truly wounded her with every refusal. Her voice grew bitter. "What on earth do you want?"

The god looked up at the rising sun and rolled his shoulders back in a shrug. "You'll have to walk home." He told her, and then he was gone.

On the third night the clearing was darker. The moon had shrunk down into a thin sliver in the overcast sky. The cloak was lying on the ground where the girl had thrown it, and a film of dew and cobwebs made it shimmer strangely against the dull, flat sand.

"Take it." Hestia said from the darkness. "Take it and go away."

He could see her when he shaped his eyes into the keen eyes of the night hunters. She wore her plain, patched clothes, and her hair was caught up in severe braids. The stink of lye and soap clung to her with the weariness of a day of hard work. Some of her nails were broken, and Kernunnos understood. Like himself, she had thrown herself into her work all day. He had stalked the realms like a feral cat, bringing down countless beasts until he could have bathed in their blood. She had worked so furiously that she had not noticed that she was grazing her hands. He saw all of this at a glance, but it was only when he stepped closer that he realised that her face was wet with tears.

"Are you crying?" He asked, idiotically. She looked up with a furious expression.

"No!"

Kernunnos studied her more closely, feeling an odd curiosity lurking in his concern. She scowled and shoved him away, but when her hands sank into his tunic she sniffled and started weeping again. The god instinctively wrapped his arm around her shoulders and wished he knew the right words to say. It would have helped to know why on earth she was crying. Such a thing had never happened around him before. He doubted that Hestia would be comforted by him asking one of his siblings for advice, and so he stayed silent.

"Three nights." The girl sniffed, and was it anger or amusement in her voice? "In the stories it's always three night. And I got three wishes, didn't I?"

"I only granted two." He offered: "I couldn't tell you why I didn't want you, because there is no way to answer an untruth."

She laughed shakily and shook her head, and somehow she was still crying. "You didn't grant the first one either. They say the crops are rotting in the fields. The animals in the forest are all sickening and starving and even the goats' milk is drying up. We could have stopped that."

For the first time he felt ashamed – truly ashamed. He cared not for his divine duties, but suddenly he cared about the handful of mortals in this cold, insignificant mountain village. They had chosen him, of all the gods, to bless their fires. As he struggled with the unfamiliar emotion, he noticed the girl's expression and realised that she might say exactly the same thing. Was she upset because she thought she had failed?

"It's not your fault." He told her. "I would not have blessed anyone."

Such selfishness was an astounding thing for a god to confess, and he felt the sting of it keenly. Hestia barely reacted to his absolution, but she caught up his hand and held it. The gesture was jarring.

She asked with her sharp insightfulness: "Are gods allowed to be so human?"

He laughed at that and shook his head. "Only if we don't get caught. We can curse a whole village, but we're not allowed to admit that we did it out of petty anger. Mortals are supposed to believe that we're stronger than that. Gods are little clockwork toys which will bless mortals if they wind us up the right way, nothing more."

"That's sad." She didn't sound convinced, but the sympathy in her voice was real enough. He shook his own head, but the gesture was far more animalistic: the wary action of a stag gauging the wind blowing through the trees. Hestia watched him with her serious, level eyes, and

Kernunnos decided it would be worse to misunderstand her than to cross some inscrutable mortal taboo.

"Why were you crying?"

She shot him a disparaging glare. The god reddened. This was probably something that he was supposed to have worked out. The woman wiped the tears from her eyes and shrugged wryly, avoiding the question.

"Will you grant me my third wish before you go?"

"Am I going?" He asked diffidently. She looked close to tears again, but before her eyes welled up she laughed and raised her chin.

"I'm fair sure you won't be coming back next year." She spoke tartly, plainly. "So you'd best go sooner and give me more time to pick mushrooms and work out how to feed a whole village with them."

The god scowled at this assault and stood up to pick up the cloak. At the very last moment he turned around to make an angry retort, and caught himself in her brilliant blue eyes, and his words choked into a bitter tirade. He told her everything that had happened with the goddess and the wretched townsfolk, and his fierce refusal to bow to any of the selfish creatures and give in to their demands.

"They had no right – no right! – to make you do it! How dare they offer you up to me like a mindless slave? They had no reason to summon me in the first place. Wanton knew that, how much I hate being twisted up in their perverted games..."

"But you're the stag." Hestia interrupted him for the first time in long minutes. Kernunnos wheeled around and snorted derisively. His eyes blazed like coals, and for the first time she took a step back and looked fearfully upon the face of the angry god.

"I hunt. I am the predator for the weak and the prey for the strong. My fires are the charnel grounds of blood and bone, not the hot earth of this barren soil. It was your kin who made me what I abhor – and your offerings which disgust me. I will not be blamed for your ignorance!" He roared this last part, but the mortal did not flinch.

"Why are you even here?" Her voice was so mulish that it broke through Kernunnos's tirade. He frowned.

"I told you. I was summoned."

"This year." She agreed. "But you were here last year, too. It was the raven's turn to be worshipped, not yours."

He flushed and kicked at the ground, looking smaller and more uncomfortable now that his immortal fury had ebbed away. The mortal smiled and stepped forward, hesitating before touching his shoulder and meeting his unsteady glare. Kernunnos shivered, thinking that mortals were terrifying in their odd certainties. This woman had barely been alive for long enough to watch a sapling grow into a tree, and yet she could see so much just by looking into his eyes.

"I knew it was you." She spoke softly. "I knew you couldn't be a traveler. I wondered if you'd been watching me... hunting me." She smiled a little then and looked down, both shy and bold. "I liked the idea."

Kernunnos did not answer. He had barely moved, but he raised one hand to where her palm touched his shoulder and traced the shape of her fingers. She blinked, looked away and then back, and blushed. A note of mischief crept into her voice, but she spoke with the same blunt pragmatism which, he realised, he was beginning to admire.

"I did not mind that they chose me for you. I was so nervous, but all of their silly chanting seemed so ridiculous that I couldn't be scared. The only thing I could think of was – would it be you? Was I right? I could have been wrong, but I did want to see you again and so I thought of that, and forgot to be scared. Then the liquor wore off and there you were! But you looked so severe and angry, and you were so rude!" She grinned as he shot her a sharp look and then shrugged. "Well, I told myself I had three days to see if you weren't a complete ass. Maybe in three hundred I could have made up my mind."

"You set a snare." He admired the ploy, respecting her as a fellow hunter. The mortal woman had moved through is mind like the simplest forest trail and set a trap with such skill that even he had blundered into it. For three nights he had told himself that she was a fool, or a tease, or a scold – all things which he knew were untrue the moment she smiled. Now it was clear that she had been testing him, searching for her own answers as avidly as he had searched for his own.

"Is that why you were crying?" He asked, "Because I was rude to you?"

She shook her head, and looked so miserable that he could not bear it, "I don't want you to go away."

Kernunnos took her hand then. He explained, very awkwardly, that he was in love with her. The girl listened in silence, and she could not meet his eyes when she admitted that she felt the same way. It was a peculiar, solemn exchange which was quietly honest on his side, and shy on hers. They sat beside each other on a fallen tree for a long time, not looking at or touching the other, until Hestia raised her head and her eyes shone with tears.

"Will you grant me my last wish, before you leave me?"

He looked around, and ran his thumb along her cheek to catch the tears before they fell. There were too many, and she was weeping for him, and his heart felt so full that he could not bear it.

"Don't forget me like the others," She begged him. Against that broken note he felt the last of his divinity crumble away. He could not be a god, not around her. He loved her as a man, with the pure dying love of the mortals, and as he folded her in his arms he knew that he would never be able to let her go.

He took her under those trees, looking into her blue eyes and feeling the gentle, shy pressure of her hands on his back, the soft sweetness of her lips on his skin. She whispered his name – his true name – and he breathed in the scent of her body and the warm, dry leaves that they crushed under their gentle dance, and if he thought of smoke and blood it was only because this was so much better.

His huntress, this creature of snares and soft words, moved under him so sweetly that he felt only love. The goddess was far away, and even when his huntress's soft lips parted in pleasure her blue eyes never clouded. She rode him, giving herself to him without letting him take, sacrificing nothing but love upon his altar until he groaned and tried to pull away, thinking to dash his seed upon the ground.

"No," She whispered, and pulled him back into her arms, her embrace. "Let this be for you."

He kissed her, felt her hands draw his against her breasts and felt himself cresting, her words burning in his blood like flames. The goddess could have claimed him then, sobbing out the mortal's name with every surge, but Hestia's shining eyes were clear and when she closed them in pleasure he knew that the feeling was her own.

They lay upon the fallow ground, still entwined, and already he wanted her again. It was the insatiable, demanding passion of the stag, and for the first time he shared his human desire with the animal part of his nature and let it roar in his blood. Hestia caught her breath at the expression in his eyes and kissed him. He felt the blessing of life stirring within her even then.

"I am sorry." She said, and when she pressed her palm to her stomach he understood that she knew too. It had taken her only a few minutes to understand what had happened. "I shouldn't have done that."

"I had no chance to argue," He smiled and raised her in his arms, brushing broken leaves from her skin and letting his hands drift over her body with unabated desire. He had never wanted a woman a second time, nor felt any need to linger after the act was done. Hestia bit her lip and thought for a moment, and then unbelievably her mischievous practicality was back and she returned his embrace.

"I'm glad. I would have argued back. I'm fair sure it's rude to argue with a fertility god about such matters on his own day." She caught his lip between his teeth and then kissed him, more passionate now that her shyness was gone. "Take me again. I know you want me. I feel like I'm glowing."

"Is that your fourth wish?"

"My only wish." She breathed, and lowered her head to kiss his throat. "If it means I can keep you."

"I am not yours to own."

"Yes, you are." The mortal woman tangled her fingers into his hair, her body rearing up in lean power like a great cat which prowled the night, fluid and dangerous in the darkness. Her eyes blazed, and in that moment she was more than his equal, more than his mate, burning with human love and divine life into something far greater than any god could ever possess. "You are mine." She spoke strongly, her soft voice rich with power. "I claim you. I own your love, your body, your heart just as you own mine. You are my offering, and I am yours until the sun burns out."

He pressed her into the ground and rose over her, lowering his head like the stag and facing her down, pressing her to yield to him, to fear him. He let her see his love for her, the danger and the pain of it, the eternity that it bound her to, and she never trembled. She returned his fierceness without fear.

"This time for the land." He growled it, and she raised her body under him to let the animal claim her, and she was not afraid of his feral nature any more than she was cowed by his love for her. The land swallowed them in dust and sand and slick, warm earth and they felt it breathe, opening itself as desperately as she had, gasping with her every breath until it was too late for the god to do anything but snarl out his release into the starving land.

The fields bore twice their crop for ten generations. Artemis was born in the spring.

CLAUSE FOR THOUGHT

A MAN ONCE DROPPED HIS FINEST COMMA
Into an Oxford brogue
He thought it just a parsing flaw
But the comma soon went rogue

It turned about, and upside down
Possessive now, it could be found
Leaving Esses quite bereft
And pluralising right and left

The man thought he would write a list
To tell the comma it was missed
He showed the world adjective sorrow
In single phrases
Short.
Hollow.

Another symbol might have found
A place betwixt his verb and noun
But the man was quite decisive:
A semicolon was divisive
Periods knew their time and place
And line-breaks took up too much space.
A comma was just meant to be
(He'd learned that at his grammar's knee)

And so the man pursued his verse
But his phrases were perverse
He claimed – in endless stilted sound –
That his comma would be found
Until one day he heard a view
That he really should have heeded
It said (in perfect English, too!)
That Oxford Commas *just weren't needed!*

SOUR

THEY TOLD ME THAT THE WORLD ENDED TEN DAYS AGO. Well, I say that they *told* me. Actually, they shouted it in the street. But why not start this story with a lie? After all, who would hold me to the truth? I might say, then, that I shouted back at them. Yes, why not? If I can pretend they were speaking to me, I can pretend that I shouted back at them, and they turned around, and were more than just strangers.

That's right: Because I shouted back, I can describe them to you. Their faces, as set with fear as their voices were rife with it. The one who laughed as he shouted would have that same manic glint in his eyes; perhaps the woman would have the traces of tears on her cheeks. Or perhaps they would both be frozen, glacial, both so full of emotion that they are quite empty. Ah yes, I know that feeling well enough to describe it to you. Even when you feel like that, your voice can still tremble, or laugh, or weep... whichever it was.

They shouted that the world had ended. We are living in the after-days, the rapture, the apocalypse. Whatever you want to call it – and I don't care, so call it what you like. The world has ended.

Which world? I thought about shouting back, and as far as you know, I did. *Whose world? Yours?*

They are still alive, after all. They can run through the streets, even if they are running *away.* They can stand in the sunlight even if it also means they have to stand in the cold wind. They have each other. They have strength enough to shout without croaking out harsh syllables, and they can probably shout in the streets for hours without needing to rest. Their world still lives.

They're obviously mad. I can't think why they are doing it. Perhaps they think that they are warning people. I doubt it. They laughed. They probably don't believe the words they're shouting. They laugh and shout because, every time the words cross their lips, they seem more real.

If they're right, then perhaps they won't live long enough to truly understand that they are going to die.

And I wonder if that is a good thing.

***

I spend a lot of my time thinking. In short bursts, of course, but I like to think it's a productive way to spend my time. I pulled back the curtains for a while to look out, to see if the strangers would come back, but it didn't take too long before the light hurt my eyes, and then my head. The street repaid me with emptiness and the sticky rot of leaves and rubbish, blown into the gutters by the wind. It doesn't take much to turn my stomach, and it takes nothing at all to make my head hurt, and so I stopped looking. If they return I'm sure I'll hear them.

But I couldn't help thinking about them. Perhaps I *should* have shouted something back.

It came to me while I slept fitfully on the sofa this afternoon. I mean, the reason came to me, in the confused way that some thoughts appear when I'm tired. The reason why those two madmen made me pause and look out of my shell of a home.

It wasn't the blind panic in their voices, or the laughter. It was the silence around them. It was the first noise I'd heard in... in I-don't-know-how-long. I hadn't even realised until they shouted that the world was so peaceful. But now my ears rang with it.

I looked out of the window again, but I couldn't see the road in the fading light. The streetlights hadn't come on yet, either. In the morning, I'll look and see if there are tire tracks in the leaves. I can't remember the last time I heard a car.

***

You must be thinking badly of me. Actually, I don't know why I said that. I only speak into this bloody cassette recorder to have someone to talk to. My counsellor used to make me record my daily routine – you know, my symptoms, when I'm tired, what I manage to do, *how does that make you feel, my dear, that's the important thing! We want to know!* Well, you know -all the bureaucratic horse-shit they make you record, as if you could reduce everything that's happening to you to a few sentences on a tape. I only stuck it out for a few months, until they started telling me how they knew me better than I did.

You don't know me, I said, *Just what I've told you, and that's not enough for you to decide.*

Are you saying you lied to us? They go cold when there's money involved, I've found. It's better to placate them. If you try to argue, even semantically, politely, rationally, calmly... well, you're too emotionally invested, surely you can see where clear eyes and a cool head are better?

You think: A cool head, cold eyes and a frozen heart, but you say yes for the fake warmth, and so you don't spend the next year trying to argue and live with nothing but dust in your bank account. But they left me the tape recorder, and I'm bloody well keeping it. Talking to it is more of a habit now, but on the off-chance that someone visits me, I like to know that my voice is still strong enough to have a natter.

Still, why would the tape cassette think badly of me? It's this apocalypse nonsense, stuck in my head and coming out of my silly mouth. I read a lot of stories. There's always some record, isn't there? You start these post-apocalyptic dystopias with someone finding a book or a recording from the before-times. It makes the story more relatable to its readers, naturally, but it gives you something else to think about. If you were recording a tape to speak to people after the end of the world, what would you want it to say?

More to the point, who would listen to it?

***

I need to stop thinking so much. The thoughts were keeping me awake. I had to take a sleeping pill in the end to chase them away, and I have precious few of any pills left. Especially if the madmen were right, and the world has actually ended. I don't suppose Boots has a post-rapture delivery service. It's certainly not mentioned on my repeat prescriptions...

When I woke up the thought was still there: *Who would listen to this?* I wonder about you. Do you know, I'm actually kind of jealous of you? You'll know what caused the end of the world, I bet. I don't. I might be the only person in the world who –literally!- managed to sleep through the apocalypse.

What was it? I suppose I'd have noticed an earthquake, or a nuclear bomb... although in this town we'd probably only get the fallout from that. I've not noticed any dust in the air, though. So it's probably not that. After those two choices my mind gets a little whimsical. I don't think I'd mind an alien invasion... they might even find me interesting enough to keep me alive, giving me enough to stay alive while they stared at me and tried to work out my worth... if their currency is in pounds sterling, it'd be pretty much the same as the old world for me. That's if they're intelligent aliens. A lot of aliens seem to just be hungry.

It could be zombies, I suppose, but I haven't noticed any shambling. The only thing that lurches and moans around here is me, but I'm usually after a cuppa, not brains. When I made my tea this morning I blearily watched the teabag bobbing in the lumpy water while my thoughts kept racing: *Mayan prophesies, comets, Revelation, plague, I wish I had fresh milk and not this dried crap...*

I might go to the store later. I'm feeling almost well today. I might not. It's better to be safe than sorry, and even if it's not the end of the world, walking to the end of the road will wear me out for the next few days.

***

The shops are closed. I came back to look at my diary. I don't think it's a bank holiday, but then I couldn't be sure. I can't find my diary. The walk has made my legs tremble, and I had to clutch at the fences on the way home. They're soft and rotting, and my fingers brushed against so much chewing gum that I started to retch. Nobody came to help me, but that's not so unusual.

The air smells odd. I haven't felt so sick in months.

I don't think I want milk in my tea after all.

SANCTION
Vivien Leanne Saunders

SANCTION

THE MOST FITTING PUNISHMENT was to bury the thing alive. There was no point in sending it away – the foul thing would return, and then what would happen? So they broke through the sewer walls and shoved the creature into the labyrinth. They threw food and beer at it and laughed when its sobs turned into snotty screams.

"Stop snivelling!" They jeered, forcing bricks back into the wall, "There are a hundred ways out! The faster you start looking for them, the sooner you'll be free!"

It snuffled and they heard it clomping away down the tunnel. It must have been pitch black, for the percussive sound faltered a few times, and they heard it cry out in shock. They laughed again and left.

They did not think that it would die. They were not wise enough to treat death as anything more than a distant, dark form who only tapped on the shoulders of people who were much older than them. Besides, they were too drunk to see the world as it truly was. They had wanted to hurt the creature for so long that they were giddy with sadistic glee.

The creature closed its eyes. Its tears were hot; the clammy air was cold. When it reached out the stone was slick and the bones were coarse. How many people had died there? Some of the skulls were deformed. Time, or infirmity, had twisted the skulls into jagged husks. The creature knew that there were rats down here. It pulled its hand away as soon as it felt softness, but the sounds of scurrying feet grew louder with each passing minute.

Minutes? Perhaps they were hours. The creature felt like days were passing. It was afraid to sleep. The rats would as soon devour a sleeping body as a dead one. It ate the bread and drank the beer until it was giddy and the bottles were empty. When the tipsy haze crept away, the creature felt cold and wet. It was raining in the world above. The water began to rise.

It saw light when it closed its eyes. It flickered red, purple, blue, gold, anything but black. Sometimes there were faces in the light. The creature recoiled from them. They had beautiful faces and shining hair. Their eyes were alive with joy. The creature loathed them with every scrap of its flesh. Even now, thinking of them, its heavy hands folded into trembling fists.

It slept eventually. The light behind its eyes grew dimmer. The bites stopped troubling it. Would it be better to starve, or to be eaten? It lapped water from the walls and retched at the slimy strands that stuck to its teeth. Life was a rancid habit. The creature only suffered because it wanted to keep walking. The liars had said that there was a way out.

It was only when it was hopelessly lost that the creature realised it could have broken down the wall. They had only stacked the bricks back the way they had found them. The creature was stronger than all of them. It had been afraid of them. The labyrinth was far more terrifying, it knew that now. It crouched down in the slime and wept.

That was when it stopped walking.

Another light blossomed behind the creature's eyes. A thin, golden thread gleamed in the darkness. The glow was so soft and sweet that the filth it illuminated looked like golden grass. The creature sighed and rested its head against the wall. It was so tired. It watched the thread scything through the labyrinth. It was death.

The golden light flicked up and dazzled the creature so much that it blocked its eyes and cried out. There was an answering cry, and death closed his hands around its shoulders.

"Anouk!" he cried. The radio at his belt crackled, and he yammered into it so quickly that the creature could not understand the rapid French.

Anouk? It was her name, the creature remembered. The liars had called her a monster. Why had she believed them?

"Thank god we found you!" the policeman took a deep breath and spat into his radio, "Theon here. Where the hell are the EMTs?" he looked at Anouk in horror. Anouk covered up her filthy face and squeezed her eyes shut.

Yes, Estelle was still there, hiding her beautiful face in the light. She had smiled at Anouk when the school bell rang. She had smiled when she offered her a ride home. She had smiled when she shoved bricks into the wall.

"My project," Anouk had said shyly that morning, "Is about the Paris Catacombs."

The classroom fell silent, waiting for the teacher to congratulate her. He always did with Anouk. Teacher's pet. He only liked her because she was fat, and ugly, and spent all her time reading books. The little cow.

Estelle raised her hand. She smiled.

"Have you ever been there?"

THE PRINCE OF TIERRA FIRMA

SHE DIED, HE SAID, FOR THE SAKE OF PURITY.

In that final hour, the word had none of the irony which it deserved. Besides, she was pure. There was no way that she could be otherwise under his tireless care. It wasn't her fault that the word was meaningless. Donna Elvira de Aguirre – 'El Pura', they should have called her, just as their christened her father 'El Loco'.

He had always searched for purity. The meaning of it changed as he grew older and more deranged - the purity of religion, perhaps, as the heathen temples were reclaimed. The purity of blood, certainly. Even when he laid claim to the throne of Spain, he did not dispute their holy right to hold on to it. But by the end of his life the purity was made of flesh and metal: the body of his daughter, and the gleaming spectre of gold.

He killed her, of course. For the want of grain and clean water, his army sickened and died. The dream of the city crumbled, and its mythical gold was forever lost. For the want of gold, he turned to his own possessions. He had slaves, a few stragglers, a boat and a daughter.

Aguirre was not a good man. When they cut his body into pieces nobody wept. Perhaps Elvira would have, if her severed throat could produce such an animal sound. She had lived well from the carrion her scavenger father had ripped from the hearts of the Aztec tombs. That was not his crime. Nor was it the taking of slaves, the incest, murder and torture which he delighted in. Those were normal enough. Aguirre roused an army against the Spanish throne – three hundred men, raising five guns against a country on the other side of the world. He invoked the name of Almighty God – ah! There it is.

That is not the whole story, but it is enough.

The gleam of gold was lost in the murky filth of the Amazon river. It trickled away as slowly as the endless hours they spent staring at the shore. The men they passed smiled and waved, and threw them darts and arrows in the same way a woman might throw a flower at a stage. The thorns pricked, and many men's hearts skipped a beat. Some stopped altogether. The ones who God did not call home were sick and frightened enough to listen to Aguirre's fevered words, and so he showed them his purity.

Gold.

The slaves pointed into the wall of trees and promised a whole city of it. Their eyes gleamed in laughter, but the soldiers saw only passion. In their world a lump of yellow metal could transform a life. If it had so little value here that whole cities could be hewn from it, then why would the natives look so enthalled? One might as well ask for bone or brick. They did not want to believe it, but they had been ordered to find it. They did not know that the expedition was meant to humour them while the politicians brokered for peace. They drank up Aguirre's stories like men dying of thirst.

Parched, on the river, they continued to die. El Pura survived before she died. Nobody ever speaks of her. She is as lost as a city of gold crumbling into the trees. Nothing beside remains.

FAMILIAR

IN THE BEGINNING THERE WAS NOTHING, AND THE NOTHING DRAGGED ITSELF INTO THE LIGHT. The nothing had not been waiting to be summoned, or slowly grown from the oily slivers of chance into a mass of cells and possibilities. There was nothing about its body which it had earned, fed, favoured or grown. It had simply sprung from the nothing into the everything.

Its body shuddered in shock, struggling and burning as it learned how to breathe. Its mouth opened in a bovine low of horror, but it could not plead for help. The nothing had not given it any words or understanding. Consciousness was abhorrent. It lay, twitching, and let experience wash over it in a scalding tide.

The man stared at the nothing curiously. In his formidable ignorance he thought that it was afraid of him. He did something – a movement of the lips which made the air tremble. The shivers passed beyond the nothing's eyes and squirmed into its ears. A hard click, a yawing caw, another click and a hiss. It closed its eyes, trembled at the darkness, and forced them open.

"Cadence." The man said again. He touched the nothing's cheek. "Your name is Cadence."

Cadence was such a tangle of limbs that it could not stand. It lolled against the man as he carried its to a chair. Gravity dragged greedily at it, and if its feet had not been wedged against the carpet it would have fallen. The man watched as Cadence, pathetically infantile, struggled to make sense of its own flesh.

Its dilated eyes fell upon disjointed shapes, and its body copied them. From the blurred images of the fireplace it constructed wooden skin, clay fingernails and hair that flickered like fire. It could not make herelf burn. Yes, there was a soft heat that suppurated the oily mess beneath its shifting skin, but however hard Cadence tried it could not will it into flames. When the man returned he cried out and made his own skin pale and moist.

Cadence mimicked its first human emotion: fear. It was not intended to be its first, and the creature felt it violating its body like the sharpest blade. It answered the man's shock with its own, rising, terror. The raw emotion screamed from its in a ghastly wail until the man cried out and fled.

The nothing could not bear his absence. There was no purpose in the world, for he had given its none, and without him it could not understand its own being. It turned its energy towards pleasing him. The temptation to drink the world around its settled into a desire to consume each part of him which he offered. It recalled his shape and, upon forming it, discovered the tensile strength of muscle and bone. It took a long time for its to drag itself to the door, but its new limbs did not falter or tremble. Its eyes could not make out colour, but now they would focus.

The man sat beside a table with his head in his hands. It recognised the small blocks around him as *books.* When it was beginning, he had held one in his hands. There were far more of them here, but he did not cling to them with the same impassioned joy. Water was seeping from his eyes, and he made a low moaning sound.

Cadence checked its shape one last time and then dragged itself over the threshold. The man's head snapped up, and his eyes narrowed. "Do you know?" he asked, and then stood to meet its. His eyes were quick and clever, and the creature immediately adopted them. He took half a step back, and then his mouth twisted, "Are you trying to look like me?"

It raised and lowered its head when he prompted its. The man breathed out in a rush, "Was the – the fire and the – was that your true form?"

The creature closed its eyes, not knowing that the world did not darken for the man as it did for its. It had never had a true form. The shape it had worn at its beginning had been his invention, not its own. As soon as his attention wavered it had worn any features which pleased its.

When it opened its eyes the man was looking down at its body, and his hands were touching its arm. Some of the awe that he had greeted its with had returned, but his voice shook as if he were laughing. "We wear clothes, Cadence. The sleeves should not be a part of your body."

He stripped his jacket off to demonstrate, and then one stockingless foot was revealed. Cadence reached out and fumbled his clothing. It was warm, and a little damp, just as his hands had been when he had carried its. For a moment its mind produced a strange comprehension of *skin,* and it forced it towards his own word, *clothes.*

There was no point changing its own body again. It had no idea what it was supposed to look like beneath the living fabric of its own clothing. It plucked at the man's shirt but his face twisted and he pushed its away. Cadence mimicked the expression and learned *laughter.*

As the days passed it worked hard on its own body, forcing itself to hold a shape for hours at a time and reminding itself to move within its limitations. Strength was easy, but balance eluded its. The man often grew impatient at its slowness and carried its back to its chair, but he was not always nearby. When the world edged closer to the darkness of the *nothing* he locked himself into another room and was silent until the sun rose.

Cadence did not sleep. It could grow weary – even exhausted – but time refreshed its as easily as slumber. The darkness of unconsciousness repelled its. Night time did not compare to the black world that had cast its out. Even when the moon was shaded, There was light.

When it could hold a form for three days and night the man began to speak. It understood the words, but each of the notions eluded its. It had no conception of life, or of purpose, or even of play or supper. It did not know how to help, hinder or hurt – despite his insistence. It only knew how to *be.*

Still, There were some details which it already knew. He said that he had called its, and it knew it to be true. His voice had dragged its from the darkness. The man tried to explain why he had done it, and in that breath he taught its how to lie.

He wanted a companion, he said. A familiar. No, he had only wanted to see if it was possible. He had meant to do something else entirely. It was an accident. A *mistake.*

Cadence smiled, because it knew this to be untrue. The darkness had spat its out in one easy moment, and in the next he had claimed its and named its. His voice had been sweet with certainty. Even though he had soured towards its, it could not forget his first, honeyed words.

The man did not tell its his own name. Perhaps, Cadence thought, it was supposed to choose one as he had chosen its own. It amused itself with the idea for several days. It only knew words that the man had spoken, since it itself could not make a sound. It tried many words in the dark–light–night, pairing them with the human face which it wore. *Table, Cup, Sit, Sleep, Listen, Stop.* None of them fit.

The man made a peculiar sound every morning when his eyes lit on its face. He told its that it was unsettling to see his own face staring back at him. "Besides," he added, turning its face from side to side, "You're female."

To show its the difference, he brought a stack of paper into the room and beckoned its over. He had borrowed the sketches from an artist, he warned its, so they must not be damaged. He sorted them into two piles: one of men, and one of women. Cadence studied both and watched the man's face as he offered its the women's pictures. His eyes lingered overlong on some of them, and it could hear his heart beating a little more quickly. The creature picked up one such image and memorised it. It closed its eyes and recreated every element. Large, almond-shaped eyes ringed by black smudges of lash. Parchment yellow skin, with a soft woven texture. Fragments of dust caught in long, charcoal locks of hair.

The man held up his hands in disgust. It was recreating a *drawing,* he cried! Couldn't it tell the difference?

Cadence lowered its head and felt its charcoal curls crumbling to dust on its cheeks. The dusty eyelashes spilled flecks into its eyes, and it felt them burn and grow moist. The man mumbled an apology and swept the drawings back into their folder.

The man was quiet for the next few days. He did not teach it more of his words, and he could not meet its eyes. Cadence was rebuffed whenever it tried to comfort him. Its confusion became frustration. If the man could not show it *female,* then how did he expect it to transform?

It stormed into the man's study one morning and tried to explain. It pointed at the fire, and its hair crackled and shone. It gestured towards the window and its skin grew as blue as the sky. He stared at its, and it pointed at him. Mimicking his face was something it could do without effort, but today it also aped his clothing and his acne, and every callous and smudge his pen had left on his hands. Finally, it poked a finger onto the folder and raised its hands in the most elaborate shrug it could summon.

The man laughed a little, and nodded. Cadence felt its anger drip away, and warm satisfaction replaced it. It was the first time that it had explained anything about itself, and the first time that he had listened. And yet, Cadence was still alive with frustration. It stared at the being that had created it and wondered – desperately wondered – how something so stupid had stumbled upon the gift of life.

Yes, he must be stupid to grant life so thoughtlessly. Cadence forced itself to smile, and learned *lying* as intuitively as it had learned *truth*. Life was easy. An accident could bring it into being.

Cadence looked at its creator and wondered if he was clever enough to send it back into the nothing. He didn't realize how close the darkness was. The creature wondered how little effort it would take to send the mortal hurtling over the edge.

There would be less in the nothing once he was inside.

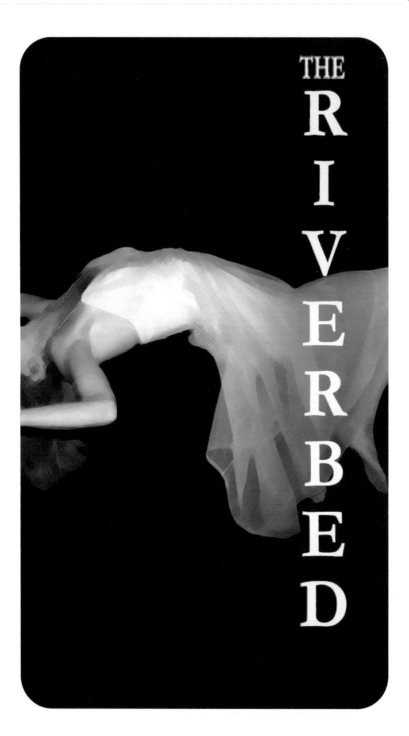

THE RIVERBED

THE RIVERBED

Preview Chapter

CLAY

I HAD BEEN DEAD FOR LESS THAN AN HOUR WHEN MY MOTHER DUMPED ME INTO THE RIVER.

The summer was so hot that sweat trickled down people's faces like rancid fat. Flies spewed from the sewers and squirmed into grey cuts of meat and jugs of sour milk. The pox closed every fifth person into its pustular embrace. A body would rot quickly in such heat, and the last thing my family needed was a rancid corpse putrefying in their kitchen. Perhaps that had been at the top of my mother's mind, or perhaps she had already done all of her grieving. I had spent weeks withering away.

I do not blame her for her mistake.

Still, she did not spare a moment to embrace her child, to whisper that she loved me or to bid me goodbye. I remember that there was only silence, and the heavy pain in my head, and then suffocating darkness as the lid of the coffin slid over me.

The river was full of grime and sewage close to the docks, but as my coffin floated downstream the water grew cool and sweet. The smell of good air and green plants revived me a little, and I felt a fine mist through the seal between the base and the lid. In her hurry, my mother had forgotten to seal the cheap coffin closed. I was lucky that the carpenter had made it well despite the rough edges; it floated as well as a boat, and carried its slight passenger in the current without a murmur.

I have no idea how long I slept for, lulled by the gentle swaying of my boat. Sometimes I was lucid, but when I forced my eyes open they stung with salt, and when I struggled to move my arms I could not reach to wipe it away.

I dread to think what would have happened if my dazed idiocy had faded away. The wooden lid was a bare inch from my nose. To this day I have nightmares about opening my eyes and seeing the close, rough grain. I never saw the inside of my coffin, and so I had no idea that I had been buried alive.

My world splintered around me.

The rocks felt too hard against my hot skin, and I feebly shoved them away until my arms broke free. The coffin cracked and shuddered, and another plank of wood groaned and drifted away. Dim sunlight burst through the gap. I recoiled from it and felt sand beneath my bare feet.

Panic gave me strength, and as more of the light spilled through the traitor coffin I dug my fingers and toes into the sand and struggled free. For a beautiful moment I was completely submerged. I felt delicious cool water sliding into my ears and my mouth. Then I opened my eyes, saw the surface shimmering above me, and choked. I pushed myself forwards and out of the wreckage onto the shore.

The sun was setting when a woman found me lying in the shallows. Her cry of disgust woke me, but I did not have the strength to look up. I felt a hand on my shoulder, and when she rolled me onto my back she grunted. My clothes were sodden and weighed my dry husk of a body down. Mother had wrapped me in my finest dress, and a thick woollen cloak, so that whatever river demon claimed me would be kind. He would know that I had been loved.

Such profound love! The stranger who pressed her hand to my nostrils cared more for me. When she felt my struggling breath against her fingertips she cursed. I heard every footstep as she stomped away. The mud made a sucking sound, and her breath rasped in her throat.

I was alone. I lay, and looked up at the stars, and my breath crackled and wheezed like the birds in the trees. It was peaceful, now that the woman was gone. I was not afraid.

The river I was lying in carried the waste from the city all the way down to the sea. The filth and rotting food bled away into the banks, and the water was clear by the time it reached the village where I had landed. The glacial beauty was deceptive. The rapid current carried the dead. There were enough hidden pools and deserted stretches for the bodies to disappear even before they were shoved out into the ocean.

The farmers and villagers buried their dead. To them, the river was not a sacred resting place, but a rotting stretch of carrion and flesh. They did not fish in it, nor drink a drop.

The river belonged to the dead. Nothing good would ever come from it.

It was no surprise, then, that my arrival caused a great deal of trouble.

Petra did not want to admit that she had been to the riverbank. The fat old shrew ran back to me ahead of the men from the village, and she pinched my ears until I started to wail.

"I heard you screaming. That's how I found you." she hissed. "If you tell them anything different I'll twist your ear right off." To prove it, she gave the lobe another sharp yank and dug her nails in. It was a particular trick she had, and when I met her husband I saw that his ears were permanently dimpled from it. Many other villagers had the same look, so I suppose the punishment was common to these people. When she backed off my headache returned with a vengeance.

"Here!" Petra cried, and made a great show of lifting me into her arms. The mud slapped onto her homespun dress, and she grunted again in distaste. Fixing her face into something like sympathy, she peered down at me and I saw her long nose, the leathery skin, and the rotting brown teeth. "There, little girl. It's alright."

"Where did she come from?" Someone demanded. Their boots paced across the dry land as they refused to come any closer.

I heard the tremor in a second man's voice. "The river spat her out."

There was a low muttering at this. Petra dropped me back into the mud. A man started shouting. He had seen the skeleton of my coffin. Heads turned to look; hearts turned to ice.

They said I had died – truly died – and that the river had sent me back. It was utter nonsense born of the stories that their grandfathers had created, and yet to my infant ears it did not seem so unlikely. I remembered dying, wasn't that true? There had been a great sense of peace, and the darkness had felt rich and thick. I could see, but not speak. That made sense too, for the dead cannot speak to the living. Through a chain of nonsense, a five year old convinced herself that she had died, and that the winnowing river had borne her into new life as gently as a mother's floating womb.

I felt sinewy arms lifting me up. The men tried to set me on my feet but I could not stand. The strength that had let me drag myself ashore had been burned away by the fever, and I hung from their arms as limply as a rag doll. Hands fell onto me, and one by one they pulled my sodden dress away until I only had my goose-fleshed skin to protect me from the night. The hands touched me again, calloused and impersonal. They turned my limbs out and around like cuts of meat, muttering to each other about every freckle and scar, until finally they were satisfied that I was not a demon.

"It does not mean that she is human." Petra dropped me back down into the mud and picked up my dress, running her calloused hands over the fine fabric. One of the men snatched it away from her and threw it into the water.

"Someone wanted the river to take her. I say we send her back." he growled. Someone laughed, and then smothered the sound with their hand. He dragged the coffin lid from the rocks and studied the rough handiwork before dumping it back into the stream. "A man made that, not a ghost. The girl is sick. Perhaps her family did not want to see her die."

There was a murmur. I have painted these men as heartless, but it wasn't quite true. They were frightened, but even cowards will not readily send a child to her death. If I was a ghost then they could abandon me without feeling a shred of guilt, but they were not so blinded by superstition that they couldn't see me shivering in the mud. Petra planted her hands on her hips and raised her voice.

"So, either someone dumped a dying brat downriver, or the river demon spat this thing into our laps to curse us. How do we decide?"

The sensible man knelt in the mud beside me. His hand touched my face, and then I felt wool tickling my skin as he covered me with his coat and lifted me up. It was the first kindness any of them had shown me, and I instinctively curled up against him as he carried me through the group.

"She needs to be fed and cared for. If you want to argue about demons then it can wait until she recovers. If she dies, at least you'll know that the river is saving its jokes for another day."

"Jokes?" Someone spluttered, and a few voices rose angrily. The man held me a little tighter, and his hand stroked my hair.

"Would you sacrifice an innocent child to your fear?" he demanded, and I felt his anger rumbling in his chest as his voice rose. "If she lives you can lock her away and inspect her flesh for any black-marks you want, but I will not let a little girl freeze to death while you argue!"

The men fell into a sullen silence, but I felt their glares burning the skin on my back.

"You'll be a wonderful nursemaid, Landen." Petra sneered. The man shook his head and I felt a sudden imbalance as he held me out to her. I whimpered, convinced I was going to fall, and he cursed and drew me closer.

"I will take her to your house, Mrs. Heim." His voice had become strangely formal. "The child needs a mother."

"I'm not the only woman in this village." she said flatly, and looked around the group. "Any of your wives could do it."

"But none of them pulled her out of the river." One of the men retorted.

She breathed out sharply through her nose and then stormed off in the sucking mud. My stomach churned as I realized that they were really going to leave me with the twisted bat. I whined and struggled until Landen understood and let me loose so I could throw up. There was nothing in my stomach, only bile, and it tasted as bitter and metallic as blood.

They say that I screamed and struggled for three days, but I cannot remember a second of it. The taste of metal stayed tart on my tongue, and every time the darkness coaxed me closer the bitterness made me shy away. The people of Singen did not make sweet things, and for those three days the women kept me alive on mushroom broth which festered in my stomach. I hated it, but my body started to heal and my stomach growled for it.

Petra rapped my knuckles with a spoon the first time I tried to snatch the bowl away. She did not see me as a child; she cared for me attentively because she relished the attention. Every animal action I made was described in garish detail to the villagers who peeked under my blankets and prodded my skin.

Petra and her husband feasted on the breads and stews which their neighbours brought so that they could gape at me. The food was filling and hearty, perfect for nourishing a sickly child. Strange, then, that I stayed thin while my nursemaid grew fat!

The more pallid and ungainly I looked, the more people gossiped. I looked like the creature they were afraid of. Petra began walking me to the fields and back each day, leaving me in the sun until my skin turned blotchy. She shaved my head bald and told the others I had been riddled with lice. She dressed me in her own clothes rather than accepting anything the other children had outgrown. With my shorn head and skinny wrists poking out of the bundled sleeves I made a convincing demon.

Singen was built from clay and stone. Its ugly buildings surrounded a slime-slick spring which dribbled out of a sheer rock face. The villagers lurked in the mountain's shadow like insects. Every man, woman and child spent their days hauling endless pails of spring water to their fields. The heavy labour gave them a peculiar appearance – short, stocky bodies with pale skin and arms that were so muscular they looked like they were wearing padded sleeves, even when they were naked. Even the children were misshapen. When my fever began to ease I thought I was still hallucinating when I saw their sickly, bulbous flesh.

A few decades ago, a distant rockslide had diverted the river into Singen. It flooded through the barren soil, carrying seeds and planting them along the banks until the land sang with life. Despite this bounty, the villagers still carried their buckets to the fields. The babbling river taunted them for it.

I only understood when I was older. The people of Singen did not read, sing, or carve. Without their work their lives were empty. If they stopped their endless toil, then their children would never understand their wasted years. How else could they respect the menial labour which had tied their ancestors to the spring?

I was a timid child, and I had never learned to disobey an adult. For a long time all I could think about was how sleepy I felt. I fell asleep in the most unusual places – at the dinner table, or into the dirty laundry pile. Once I lay myself down on the grass beside the field and, when I woke up, found an enormous thistle prickling my bottom. When the urge to sleep took me I would not have cared if my bed was on fire.

Petra never asked me for my name. I spent a month being called girl without feeling its loss, but when I was stronger I wondered if she knew what I was called. I knew I had a name, for nobody would have dressed their daughter in such a fine burial costume without calling her something, but I hadn't heard the word in so long that I had forgotten it. A score of names flew through my mind, but none of them seemed to fit. I could have been called Meera, or Sylvia, or Teresa, but then so could my sister, or even my mother. I puzzled over it until my head hurt, and decided that if anyone wanted to give me a name I would use it. Maybe, one day, someone would give me back the one that I had lost.

Sure enough, the villagers invented a name so they knew who to gossip about. The ones who liked me called me River, as if I could repay my debt to the dreary current by carrying its name on my lips. The ones who hated me called me Clay. I suppose one name is as good as another, but some spark of stubbornness made me adopt the second one. They meant it as an insult; I wore it with pride. The visiting neighbours winced when I greeted them with it. Petra refused to call me any name at all.

I dreamed of my home every night. Slowly, the fishy stench of my city was eclipsed by the musk of mushrooms and moss. When the autumn leaves began to fall I had forgotten it entirely. My family's faces took longer to die. One morning I awoke with my hands fisted at my eyes, pressing the lids into darkness as I desperately clung to one last dream. I knew that when it faded, I would have entirely forgotten that life. I rubbed my eyes until they stung with blue stars and red candle flames, and the shadow of my mother withered into ashes.

To this day the desperation of my five-year-old self still makes me catch my breath. When I was older I returned to the city, and my feet found their way onto a familiar street. I knew that I had stepped on the round, dry cobblestones before – but every house looked the same, and even if my family still lived there I would not have known which door to knock upon.

But none of that mattered to the child who sobbed her infancy into dust. Petra was awoken by my cries – great, heaving sobs, they were, sucked in through a gaping mouth – and she promised to give me something real to cry about. I bit back my wailing, pressing my hand to my hitching chest. I vowed to myself that I would never give Petra the satisfaction of making me cry. I wept for my mother, not for this hag. I could not remember the woman who had buried me, but I could feel her love in my sorrow.

***

WANT TO READ ON?

The Riverbed is due to be released in 2020-2021. Subscribe to our mailing list to find out more!

***

MORE SNEAK PEEKS AND SHORT STORIES ONLINE AT

https://sivvusleanne.wixsite.com/authorvls

If you enjoyed this book, please review it on Amazon!

FIRST EDITION – AUGUST 2019

Printed in Great Britain
by Amazon